First published by Parragon in 2010
Parragon
Queen Street House
4 Queen Street
Bath BA1 1HE, UK

ISBN 978-1-4075-3659-0
Printed in China

DISNEP
fairies

TinkerBell
AND THE
GREAT FAIRY RESCUE

PaRragon

Bath New York Singapore Hong Kong Cologne Delhi Melbourne

Tinker Bell and her fairy friends from Pixie Hollow were on their way to bring summer to the mainland!

Summer needed the fairies' constant attention – which meant that Tink was going to be on the mainland for months instead of days. She was very excited!

Tink and her friend Terence, a dust-keeper fairy, landed in a clearing.

Tinker Bell looked around the peaceful meadow. "Where is everyone?"

"Tink," said Terence, "fairy camp is in here." He walked over to a huge oak tree and pulled back a thick tangle of leaves.

"Wow!" cried Tink. Hidden beneath the tree, an entire fairy community bustled with activity.

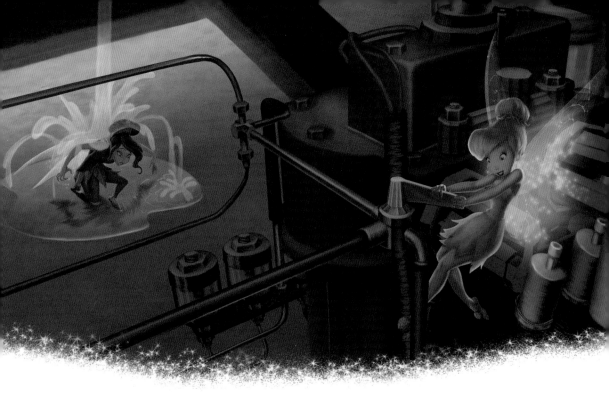

Just then, a loud **CRACK!** went through the fairy camp!
Fawn knocked over some paint that fairies were using to
decorate butterfly wings, and the splattered butterfly took off.

The loud noise made Tinker Bell very curious.

The other fairies hid, but Tinker Bell just had to see what
had made the noise. Vidia chased after her, trying to get her to
come back. Tink ignored her and flew down to examine the car
after the humans had gone into their house.

"This is amazing!" Tink said. "Those wheels back there move
because this chain thing rotates. . . ."

Tinker Bell darted inside the engine. She found an interesting
looking lever and turned it over and over again. Outside the
car, each turn of the lever showered Vidia with water!

Tink flew back out and looked Vidia up and down. "You're all
wet," she remarked.

Just then, the door to the house opened and out walked Lizzy and her father, Dr Griffiths.

Tink and Vidia froze, but they didn't need to worry. The humans' attention was focused on a butterfly.

"The wings have two entirely different patterns," Dr Griffiths observed.

"Well, I guess that's just the way the fairies decided to paint it," Lizzy said.

"Fairies do not paint butterfly wings, because as you know, *fairies are not real*," her father declared.

If Vidia hadn't stopped her, Tinker Bell would have flown out and proven that fairies existed right then and there!

Meanwhile, Lizzy was playing with a small house she had built. "Would you like to help me with it?" she asked her father.

"I'm sorry, dear," Dr Griffiths said. "I have to present my exhibit to the museum tomorrow. Now run along . . . "

Tink and Vidia were exploring. "Wow!" exclaimed Tink. She landed next to a row of buttons lined up like stepping stones. "These will be perfect for the new wagon prototype I've been working on."

"I'm not carrying this human junk back to camp . . ." began Vidia, but then she spotted something that made her stop in her tracks. It was Lizzy's fairy house.

Vidia wanted to leave, but Tinker Bell headed straight for the house!

Tink went inside of the house, ignoring Vidia's warnings that humans could be dangerous. Frustrated, Vidia whipped up a gust of wind that slammed the door shut.

Tink didn't mind. She was having fun exploring the tiny house's gadgets.

Suddenly, Vidia saw a human approaching in the distance. She pulled on the door to let Tink out, but it was jammed shut!

Lizzy went to pick up her fairy house, and was amazed to see a tiny fairy inside. Finally, she had proof that fairies were real! She started running back to her home, while Tinker Bell bounced around inside of the fairy house.

The little girl went upstairs to her room, and peeked in the fairy house. But Tinker Bell was nowhere to be seen.

"Where have you gone?" wondered Lizzy. She took the roof off the house and *ZIP!* Tink darted out.

Mr Twitches, the family cat, immediately lunged for the fairy.

As a horrified Vidia watched at the window, Lizzy put Tinker Bell in a birdcage for safe keeping.

Vidia knew she had to free Tinker Bell, but she couldn't do it alone. She flew back to the fairy camp to get help.

She explained to her friends what had happened – but a storm had just erupted.

"We can't fly in the rain," Fawn reminded her. "And the meadow's already flooded!"

Clank and Bobble had a plan. They were going to build a boat!

Back at the country house, Lizzy let Tinker Bell out of the cage.

"You don't have to be scared," said Lizzy. "I'm very nice. Look, I've been drawing fairies all my life."

Tinker Bell was amazed by Lizzy's fairy collection. But as Lizzy described what was going on in each picture, Tink realized the little girl had her fairy facts all wrong!

Tinker Bell pointed to the window.

"You want to go?" asked Lizzy. "I understand." She went to the window and opened it wide.

Tink made it as far as the windowsill and stopped. It was pouring outside!

"Can't you fly in the rain?" guessed Lizzy. "You can stay with me until it stops. Then you can teach me more about fairies!"

Back on the fairy boat, the rescuers were in a panic. They were headed straight for a waterfall!

Thinking quickly, Vidia hovered in front of the boat and created a burst of wind. The boat started to turn around!

Then suddenly, several large raindrops soaked Vidia's wings and she had to stop. The boat was swept towards the falls again.

"Hang on, we're going straight down!" yelled Bobble.

At the last second, Silvermist made water rise up so that the drop wasn't as steep. The boat crashed onshore, but the fairies were all right!

"I guess our sailing days are over," said Bobble.

Back at the house, Tink and Lizzy created a Fairy Field Guide, filled with information about the world of fairies.

By the time they were done, the rain was letting up. Tinker Bell and Lizzy both realized it was time for Tink to go home. As much as she was going to miss the little girl, Tink was really excited to get back to her fairy friends.

But as Tinker Bell was flying away from Lizzy's house, she saw the little girl trying to show her father the Fairy Field Guide. Dr Griffiths was too busy trying to fix the leaks in their home to listen to Lizzy. Tinker Bell watched Lizzy walk sadly away from her father. Tink realized she had to find a way to bring father and daughter together and make them happy again.

Lizzy thought Tink had left, but to Lizzy's surprise, Tinker Bell suddenly appeared. The look of joy on Lizzy's face let Tink know that coming back had been the right thing to do.

Lizzy went to sleep, and Tinker Bell watched as Dr Griffiths came up to check on her. "There just aren't enough hours in the day," he said to his daughter. It warmed Tink's heart, and she felt even stronger about finding a way to help them.

Meanwhile, the other fairies were continuing their mission to find Tink on foot. Vidia spotted the muddy road that led to Lizzy's house. Vidia helped her friends across, but then got stuck in the mud herself. Silvermist, Fawn, Rosetta and Iridessa grabbed onto her and pulled, but she wouldn't budge.

The fairies saw a car coming at them, but Iridessa was able to save them by reflecting the light from the car. The driver got out of his car. "Hello? Is somebody out there?" he asked.

Fawn grabbed his shoelace and instructed the others hold on tight. When the driver turned to leave, they were all pulled out of the mud!

Back at the house, Tinker Bell had an idea! She secretly fixed all of the leaks in the house for Dr Griffiths.

Before she returned to Lizzy's room, she couldn't help but notice the butterfly fluttering in a jar on Dr Griffiths's desk. It made Tink feel terrible to see the poor creature trapped and helpless.

Lizzy went to show her father the fairy book. When she reached her father's office, Lizzy could see that Dr Griffiths was upset about something.

"The butterfly is gone," he announced. "There is no one else in this house, there's only one logical explanation. It must have been you."

"I didn't," replied Lizzy. "It must have been . . ."

"It must have been who?" Dr Griffiths asked.

"I could tell you, Father," Lizzy declared. "But you wouldn't believe me."

"Very well," Dr Griffiths said, "off to your room. I'm very disappointed with you."

Back in Lizzy's room, Tinker Bell was apologizing for getting the little girl into trouble.

"I'm glad you're here," Lizzy told Tink. "You're my best friend. I wish I were a fairy just like you. Then I could fly around with the other fairies all the time."

That gave Tinker Bell an idea! She instructed Lizzy to close her eyes and spread out her arms. Then the fairy hovered above Lizzy's head and showered it with pixie dust.

Downstairs, a door creaked open.

"All clear," announced Iridessa. The fairies entered the kitchen.

"Okay," began Vidia. "Tinker Bell is upstairs. The little girl has her in a cage. There's also a large human in the house who doesn't like creatures with wings."

The fairies looked at each other in alarm.

"Great!" Fawn exclaimed. "Anything else?"

But before Vidia could reply, the fairies had their answer.

Mr Twitches was standing in the doorway!

Meanwhile, Dr Griffiths heard strange noises coming from upstairs.

"What's going on in here?" Dr Griffiths demanded when he went to investigate.

Lizzy tried to act normal, but the pixie dust hadn't worn off yet. She had to hold onto the furniture to stop herself from floating off the floor.

"How did you get footprints on the ceiling?" her father continued.

"Well, I . . ." began Lizzy. "I was flying. My fairy showed me how."

While the other fairies distracted Mr Twitches, Vidia headed to save Tinker Bell. Vidia got there just as Tink revealed herself to Dr Griffiths. He tried to catch Tink, but Vidia pushed her out of the way! Dr Griffiths ran out of the house with Vidia. "I must get this to the museum right away!" declared Dr Griffiths as he dashed down the stairs.

The other fairies had tamed Mr Twitches with some catnip
that Rosetta and Fawn found. They rode on the now friendly
cat and entered Lizzy's room. Tinker Bell and Lizzy were trying
to figure out how to get Dr Griffiths to release Vidia.

"We can't fly," said Tink, "but I think I know somebody who can."

Lizzy was nervous as the fairies bundled her up in a rain slicker and hat. "Floating around my room is one thing," she told Tinker Bell, "but flying all the way to London . . ."

The fairies swirled around Lizzy and showered her with pixie dust.

"All aboard!" cried Tinker Bell.

Tink settled under Lizzy's collar while the other fairies tucked themselves into her raincoat pockets. Lizzy had a rough start, but was soon maneuvering smoothly above the country road that led to the city.

A little while later, the magnificent sight of London came into view.

Once they got closer, Tinker Bell flew into the car's engine and brought the car to a stop.

"Father!" Lizzy called. Dr Griffiths turned to see his daughter flying towards him, pixie dust trailing behind her.

Dr Griffiths couldn't believe his eyes! "How are you doing that?" he asked. "There's no feasible scientific explanation. It has to be . . . magic."

Lizzy smiled. "It is magic," she told him.

"But where does it come from?" Dr Griffiths wondered.
"Fairies," answered Lizzy matter of factly.

Then Lizzy told her father that they had to take the fairies
back to the country. Seeing Lizzy and the other fairies, her
father understood. Seconds later, Vidia was reunited with
her friends.

Days later, Tink and Vidia sat together, sipping their tea.
Not only did they know each other better now – but they had
actually become good friends.

As they watched Lizzy and Dr Griffiths, they could see that
father and daughter were getting to know each other better, too.

"Beautiful sight, isn't it?" asked Vidia.

"Nothing more beautiful in the whole wide world,"
Tink agreed.